An Unfortunate Memory

Maddi Hartley

Copyright © 2012 Maddi Hartley
All rights reserved.
ISBN: 0615632157
ISBN-13: 978-0615632155

To my family.

4

PART ONE

6

1

It's dark again. It seems like it's always dark in these places. I should know. I've been to enough of them over the last few years. Well, more like the last couple. I haven't exactly been in this business all that long. But it's been long enough for me to remember more than I should.

The flickering candles are perhaps the only new aspect to the situation. Normally, it's just one little lamp, suspended above my head. I glance upward for a second, as though it'll be there, hanging above me. I'm actually slightly surprised when it's not, the empty space above me uncomfortably unfamiliar. I bring my head down slowly. My eyes wander around my desk, skipping over the familiar cups of lukewarm coffee and half-hearted doodles crumpled up around a yellow notepad. I stare at the notepad for a moment. It's been four hours and I haven't written a single thing. But what can I write? "Subject (f) has been sitting in corner for over four hours. May have shifted foot." That just sounds lame. I should be able to write more, I should have more to say about her. But honestly, I just can't bring myself to do it. To remember. It took me years to block all that from my mind. I don't feel like dragging it back to the light at this point.

2

It's been five hours now. Any of my colleagues would have thrown in the towel for the day at this point. I'd like to say I'm the type who refuses to give up but that wouldn't exactly be true. I'd say I'm just stubborn at times and maybe a little hardheaded. It's probably more of a pride issue, the reason I haven't left the room yet. I'm getting pretty close to turning in for the day though. Maybe I should take a bathroom break. I mean, she hasn't moved for five hours. What are the chances that she'll have a major breakthrough in the ten minutes it'll take me to run to the bathroom and grab another coffee? I'm not a betting man but I'm pretty sure the odds are in my favor. Just to be safe, I stretch slowly in my chair. I'm met with nothing. No movement from the corner. I allow myself a small grin and start to rise. Just as I'm turning to move towards the door, my eye catches something. A twitch. I freeze, my heart suddenly much louder than before. I turn slowly towards the corner. A second later, I wish I hadn't.

3

Slumped over in my chair, I can feel myself drifting into sleep. I shake myself slightly and straighten my back. I sneak a glance over to the corner again. She's not looking at me anymore. Just staring at her feet. I never thought I'd see those eyes again. I can't say I wanted to either. Just reading her name in the case file was enough to bring back memories.

Wait, no, I'm not going to think about that right now.

I rub my temples to try and clear my head. I look quickly at my watch for distraction. It's been over eight hours now. Dropping my head into my hands, I can feel the weight of the day beginning to settle across my shoulders. I feel like screaming out of frustration. I know there's nothing I can do to help her but I can't just leave her in this situation. I know too well the effects of walking out on someone. My mother was a living, breathing example of the consequences of abandonment. Sexually assaulted at the age of fourteen, my mother found herself pregnant and homeless, her father having disowned her. For a few years, she found work as a prostitute and went through two more pregnancies, each time left on her own. Then, when she was about to give up hope, she met my father. Big mistake. From what little my mother told us about him, I got the idea that he was pretty much synonymous with the devil as far as she was concerned. The gist of what I got from her rages was that he conned her into thinking he loved her, she fell for it and then he bailed a few months after I was born. She never quite recovered from that. And she never let me forget it. I barely have any fond memories of childhood. Being raised by a single mother and three older brothers in a gritty shack in a small, rural town is not exactly the most encouraging environment for a boy.

As the youngest, I was dealt perhaps the worst hand of anyone I've ever known. Because, in my family, "youngest child" is synonymous with "fresh meat". To be fair, I definitely looked the part. Skinny, pale and drowned in my brothers' oversized clothes, I epitomized the poor gutter boy my brothers worked so hard to beat down. My desire to learn didn't do me any favors either. I remember the first time my brothers found me scrounging for old newspapers, attempting to learn my letters. I was crouched behind a trash bin trying to make sense of the titles of the articles. Suddenly, a voice crept over the top of the can.

"Hey Miiikey." I froze as I recognized my brother's familiar greeting. I remained frozen as I felt the trashcan pushed to the side. The newspaper was ripped from my hands.

"What the hell's this?" my brother Mark asked. I kept my mouth shut, hoping it was a rhetorical question. It wasn't.

"I asked you a question," he growled, hitting me over the head with the paper.

"I'm trying to read," I squeaked, hands over my head.

"What?" said Mark in a dangerously quiet voice. I didn't get a chance to answer. I cowered as punches and kicks rained down on me. My brother was laughing cruelly.

"You nerd. You don't know how to read," he jeered. My other brothers joined him in laughing.

"You're a loser," he taunted between punches. "A poor, pathetic, weak loser." He stopped his assault, breathing heavily.

"This," he said, holding up the newspaper, "is garbage. You don't know how to read and you never will." He tore the paper into several pieces and threw them over my head. He laughed again, one short bark, and walked away, leaving me curled up on the ground. After a few moments I uncoiled slowly and started gathering the scraps of paper. I laid them on the ground and started to piece them back together.

4

I tried to find places where I could be alone to read. They never lasted because my brothers would always manage to hunt me down. The longest I was ever able to stay in one place was two months. That was at the library and I'm pretty sure the reason my brothers didn't find me sooner was only because they didn't know what a library was.

The library was where I really learned to read. I started by sitting in on some of the children's classes then had the librarians read titles of books to me. I was small enough that I could pass for a much younger age so they never asked any awkward questions.

Until my brothers found me, I would spend up to six hours a day in the library. I enjoyed it there because it was quiet and serene. Not like at home. Here no one asked you any nosy questions. No one cared what you were doing so long as you weren't causing a disturbance. Those two months were the closest to heaven I think I have ever been.

But before too long, I was found out. My brothers managed to corner me outside the library one day. To be honest, they might not have found me if I hadn't made so many mistakes. My first was staying at the library longer than I normally did. My brothers began to wonder where I was and went hunting. My second mistake was using the front door of the library when I usually go out through the back. Whether it was bad timing on my part, luck on my brothers or something planned by them, I basically walked straight into their arms.

"Hey Miiikey, where have you been?" That's when I made my final mistake, when I heard my brother's voice. I tried to turn around and run away. I didn't get very far. When my brothers were through with me, they had to drag my limp body home. I never dared to go back.

Of course that wasn't the only time my brothers beat on me. I don't remember ever going out without a collection of bruises across my body. Although I suppose I'm being slightly unfair to my brothers. They were very protective of me in some ways. They never let anyone else have a go at me. I remember the time some local thugs tried to mess with me, when I was six or seven years old. My brothers came out of nowhere and gave those guys a piece of their minds. As the thugs stumbled off, my older brother shouted after them.

"That's our brother, we're the only ones who get to beat on him. You got me?" I think that was one of the only times I felt proud to be a member of the Amherst family. Of course my brothers proceeded to "teach me not to talk to strangers" (in the words of my brother Mark), but it wasn't as bad as normal. I remember feeling strangely happy that day. True, it was a perverted happiness, but happiness all the same.

Unfortunately, that didn't last long. My brothers slowly built up a reputation and then no one dared to mess with me. It was a small town, where we grew up, so most everyone had heard of our family. Soon my brothers felt a responsibility to keep me in my place. Oftentimes, I was woken up with a fist to the face or the gut, followed by a shove out of my bed onto the floor. I just tried to curl into the fetal position and wait until they'd had their fill. One day, my brothers got a little carried away, which resulted in me being unable to move from that position for the rest of the day. I still have some of the scars. I have scars from almost everything my brothers did to me. I blame my mother for this, mostly. It's not like she ever tried to protect me. In fact, she encouraged my brothers to keep up their daily beatings.

"It'll make you stronger," she said in response to my cries for help. "Just look at your brothers, Michael. They know how to defend themselves." Classic Abby Amherst. I can still remember the venom in those words. It came from her memories of my father. I was a constant reminder of the pain she felt when all the men in her life abandoned her. In a sick, twisted way, I think that's why she decided to stay a parent and raise my brothers and I. Because she believed we would never leave her, never desert her like everyone else had. But just because she decided to take care of us didn't mean she had to like us. Her sons were her outlet for all her anger and bitterness at the world. That's what having children meant to my mother: a way to dump all her problems on someone else. I'm sure my mother would be as backwards a parent now as she was back then. But that was my mother, always the fighter. Always—until my brothers landed themselves in prison.

5

I'm not even sure how long it's been now. I gave up keeping track as soon as I hit ten. Hours, that is. But I can't exactly rush someone who's been catatonic for two years now. I wonder what it's like for her, trapped in her own mind with the memory of that day. It's uncomfortable for me to think about and I wasn't even there. After what she saw, I'm not surprised she wanted to run away from reality. The only problem is what she took with her when she left. That's the only reason I'm here. It's the only reason the four others before me were here as well. She's the only witness, the only person who knows what happened the day her family died.

6

I remember wanting to run away from reality—reality being my family. It was around my fifteenth birthday. I'd always dreaded my birthdays when I was a child and I'm still not very fond of them today. Because I never got presents for my birthday or any special treatment from my mother like my brothers did. The only "gift" I got was that it was the only day my brothers wouldn't touch me, the only day I could be sure I wasn't going to get attacked. They saw it as a way to let me see how lucky I was to have survived another year. I saw it as a reminder of the hell I was going to have to go through before the next birthday. When I turned fifteen, I realized that I'd had enough. Normally, I would just sleep through the whole day, dreaming of a life without my brothers, but not this year. This year I was determined to do something about it. So instead of hiding beneath my covers, I came up with a plan. The day before, while my brothers were out causing trouble, I packed what little I owned and stowed it outside our shack, near the back fence. That night I stole a handful of my mother's "emergency money"—kept safe in a jar under her bed—and left. I don't remember ever looking back. I'm not even sure if my mother bothered to look for me when she found out I was gone. She must have assumed I'd come back once the money ran out. And I would have, if I hadn't met old man Grumman on the side of the highway.

7

Meeting Grumman was probably the luckiest day of my life. And the most surreal. I mean, how many people would pick up a teenage boy off the highway? I'm lucky no one decided to run me over. I almost thought the old man was some crazy undercover police officer. I'm glad I decided to trust him, though. Thanks to him, I was able to leave my past behind and start a new life. I'd never have made it through school without old man Grumman.

I remember the day he picked me up because it was the first time I ever saw a limo. The thing pulled up alongside me and nearly gave me a heart attack. I thought I was hallucinating. And when the door opened to an old, white-haired millionaire inviting me to come inside, I think I passed out for a second or two. I debated running away as fast as I could. But the promise of shade and air conditioning won me over. As I clambered uneasily into the backseat, I remember cringing when I sat on the leather cushions, thinking of the dirt and grime I was getting all over them. The man just watched me with a strange smile on his face. As the car started moving again, I determinedly stared anywhere but at him. He was the one to speak first.

"So," he said and it wasn't a question so much as a statement. I still refused to make eye contact. I found myself looking at my reflection in the window. I barely recognized my own face. My skin, which was normally pale, had a thick layer of dirt and grime coating it. My dark brown hair had been nearly bleached blond by the sun and it hung down to my shoulders in a tangled mass. My eyes were my only recognizable feature, a bright blue inherited from my mother. I had to stop myself from reaching up to touch my face just to make sure I wasn't dreaming. I was about to examine the rest of my body when I heard a peculiar clinking sound behind me. I turned, finally, to look at the old man. He was holding out a glass of water.

"Ice or no ice?" I shook my head slowly and accepted the glass from him. It sat in my lap for a little while. The old man chuckled.

"It's not poisoned you know," he said, "and I'm no cop." I nodded and tried to swallow, which was difficult because my throat had taken on the consistency of dried plaster. I took a sip of the water then downed the whole glass. The old man smiled again and held out a bottle of water. I grabbed that and threw it down too.

"I'm going to guess you've been out in the heat for some time now," he said, watching me carefully, "and I'm also going to guess that you weren't out there on accident." I glanced at him out of the corner of my eye. He was still smiling but a different look had crept into his eyes, something I couldn't place.

"You want to tell me why?" he asked. I sat there for a moment.

"I ran," I whispered after several seconds of silence. I turned away from him again; his smile was making me uncomfortable.

"Well you must have come from someplace pretty down in the dumps to prefer wandering around the highway," he commented, handing me another bottle of water. I nodded slowly and said hoarsely, "Not too pleasant." He kept smiling and picked up the intercom.

"Hey Max," he said—to the driver, I supposed—"skip the meeting. It seems I've become otherwise engaged." He replaced the phone and looked back at me. This time I met his eyes with my own, trying to figure out what was going on inside his head.

"So," he began, "let me see if I've got this right. You've run away from a terrible place and you'd do anything to stay away from there, even if that means wandering around on the highway probably suffering from extensive dehydration and heat exhaustion."

I blinked again and nodded, adding softly, "I haven't eaten for a few days either."

The old man sighed, the smile finally fading from his face. He closed his eyes for a moment. I sat in silence for a bit, trying hard not to fidget. After a couple minutes, he laughed and raised his head. The grin was back, full strength.

"That settles it then!" he exclaimed, rather loudly for such a small space. "You're just going to have to deal with living with me from now on." I'm pretty sure my mouth dropped open. Whatever my face did, it sure made the old man laugh.

"Ah, you'll get used to it," he said, "and it's been getting pretty lonely in my house. I could use a new acquaintance. My name's Grumman." He stuck out his hand, which I shook reluctantly. His smile widened. I chanced a slight grin myself.

"This is going to be fun," he said.

8

She's still not moving. If I wasn't able to see her blink every now and then, I'd be pretty sure she was dead. I feel my body shifting involuntarily, as if it's compensating for her immobility. Glancing at my watch again, I realize how much time I've wasted caught up in memories. I shake my head and sigh. I swore I'd never think about this stuff again. Shows you how good I am at keeping promises.

9

Old man Grumman was truly a gift from god. He didn't ever ask much about my life, just made sure I was comfortable, knew the ground rules and put me through school. Eventually, I shared my story with him but I never asked why he chose to take me in. I was too embarrassed to bring it up. In fact, it was the old man who eventually broached the subject.

It was during one of my graduate school breaks, sometime in the fall. I had come home to visit for a few days. Grumman was near the end of his life at this point so I mostly kept to myself. One evening, however, he called me into his study. He was lying on his bed, eyes shut. I sat awkwardly in the chair by his side, waiting for him to speak. Finally he opened his eyes and turned to look at me.

"Michael," he said and I was shocked by how faint his voice was. He chuckled.

"I guess I'm in pretty bad shape, huh?" he commented. "Ah well, old age and not enough exercise I suppose." He chuckled again but it soon gave way to coughing. I wasn't sure whether I was expected to do anything to help. I sort of patted him on the shoulder then felt a little lame. He batted my hand away.

"Don't worry about me," he grumbled. I opened my mouth then closed it again. He noticed and waited for me to speak.

"It's about time I started worrying about you," I said quietly. "After everything you've done for me." He smiled but I couldn't bring myself to return it.

"Something bothering you?" he asked. I shrugged my shoulders, not wanting to bring it up, not wanting to sound ungrateful. Unfortunately, despite his age, the old man was pretty sharp.

"You want to know why I did all this for you," he said, and it wasn't a question but a statement. I stared at my knees sheepishly. His hand found my shoulder.

"Ah, Michael," he said, "you don't need to feel guilty for my sake. If you want to know, just ask."

"Okay," I said to my lap, "why did you take me in then? I mean, it's crazy taking someone off the highway then giving them all…this." I tapered off, unsure of how to continue or whether he had something to say. He nodded to show he understood I wasn't finished yet.

"I just," I struggled to find the words. "I just...I never asked...because...because it felt rude. I mean you gave me a whole new life and all I could think was 'What's the catch?'"
There was a long silence.

"I know how you feel," he said finally. "I'd feel the same way if I were in your shoes." He paused to take a sip of water from a glass on his bedside table.

"To be honest, I wasn't really sure why I was taking you in either at first," he continued. "I suppose I just have a weakness for types like you. I'm a sucker for those charity people always asking for money. I know you weren't asking," he said, noticing my body stiffen at the words, "but I felt bad for you. I saw you walking on the side of the highway looking so thin and tired, I at least had to give you a ride to wherever you were going. And when I saw your face for the first time, well, I saw a determination you don't see every day. And call me eccentric, but I was damn well sure I wasn't going to let someone like that waste away to nothing." I sat extremely still as the pressure on my shoulder increased. Grumman was struck by another coughing spell. When he surfaced, he shifted in bed to turn towards me.

"Michael," he said. "Look at me." Reluctantly, I removed my gaze from my knees. His eyes were starting intently at my face.

"I did not take you in and give you all 'this' because I felt sorry for you," he said. "That may have been why I pulled over on the highway, but it wasn't the reason I took you in. I took you in because I saw too much of my brother in you." I must have looked confused because the old man's face softened a bit.

"I never told you," he explained, "but when I was sixteen, my older brother ran away from home. Now we weren't raised in anything close to the environment you were, but my brother was a passionate and determined human being, perhaps a bit too hardheaded for his own good, and my parents were a tad too controlling in his mind.

"He was a bright student and would become absorbed in new ideas every day. He told me his dream was to become a rocket scientist or an engineer. My parents had other plans. They pushed him to apply for law school, the same one my father went to actually. He refused to apply. They refused to pay for anything other than a degree in law. Well, my brother wasn't the type to give up on his dream so he left. Just walked out the door one day and never looked back." I shifted uncomfortably.

"Well, he ended up in much the same place you did. Broke and homeless, wandering the streets. I found him one day, a few weeks after he ran out. I tried to convince him to come home. He wouldn't listen. He told me to go home and, like a fool, I listened to him. I thought about him the entire night and decided I was going back the next day to try again. The next morning, police were at our door asking my parents to identify my brother's body. He'd been hit by a drunk driver while trying to hitchhike." The old man stopped suddenly and turned his head away for a moment. I looked back down at my knees, trying to ignore the slight sniffling sound coming from his direction.

"Anyway," he continued after a minute, "I never forgot my brother, his determination to follow his dreams, make his life better. And when I saw you, I saw my brother the day before he died. You may have been beaten down but you weren't broken yet. And I wasn't going to make the same mistake twice. I saw you as a chance to make amends for not being able to save my brother. I hope you don't mind me using you." I shook my head slowly, my vision blurring. Grumman sighed and removed his hand from my shoulder. He settled back into the pillows and closed his eyes. A smile spread across his face.

"You're a good kid, Michael," he whispered. "Don't ever forget that." I waited for him to say something else but he'd fallen asleep. I got up quietly and left the room, wiping my eyes. That was the last time I saw the old man alive.

10

When Grumman passed, I didn't speak at the funeral. I almost couldn't bring myself to go. I'd already gone through college and most of grad school by that point and our last conversation was still too fresh in my memory. The only thing I remember clearly from the funeral was a man in a business suit—I later found out he was Grumman's personal lawyer—handing me a sealed envelope. I went home after the service, put the letter on my counter and forgot about it for a couple weeks.

About fifteen days after the funeral, I remembered the envelope. When I opened it, I found a letter from the old man detailing everything he'd managed to find out about my family after I ran out. That surprised me. I'd never even told him I worried about my mother and brothers.

According to Grumman's letter, a few months after I ran out, my brothers attacked a group of privileged kids. They had been bad-mouthing my family's way of life and my oldest brother, Mark, didn't appreciate it. He decided to have a word with them. My other brothers, Shane and Kevin, decided to follow along. Things went downhill fast. From what the old man could find out, they killed two of the kids on the spot, seriously injured a third and let the fourth one escape with a couple of broken bones. The cops didn't take long to show up. Within about two weeks, Mark was charged with second-degree homicide and given two life sentences in prison. Shane and Kevin were charged as accessories to murder and given, each, one life sentence in prison. Not all of them made it. From what I know today, only Shane survived. Kevin got caught up in a fight and had his neck snapped about two years into his sentence. Mark held on for six until he decided taking his own life was the better option. Mark's suicide was the final straw for my mother. Apparently she went insane and burned our old shack to the ground. As far as Grumman knew, she was still on the run, drifting from place to place, never staying more than a few days in one location and turning to thievery to get by. I remember shaking my head, not at the fact that my mother was now a vagrant thief but at the lack of surprise I felt learning about everything she'd done.

11

I realize I've drifted off again. Shaking myself, I reach for the lukewarm coffee and take a sip. Disgusting, but it's all I've got, I suppose. I look over to the corner. Now she's tracing some sort of circle on the floor with her finger. I wonder how long she's been doing that. I consider getting up to see if it means something but I don't really think I'll find anything interesting or helpful. Her eyes are still focused on her feet, though they might be following the circle too. I stare at what I can see of her face for a moment then my gaze moves down to the circle. Then immediately back up. But I'm no longer staring at her eyes.

I'm watching her mouth because for the first time in two years she's actually forming words.

12

I've been in this place for fifteen hours now, and I'm getting tired of staring at the same four dark walls. At least I've discovered I can get up and move around without disturbing her. Stretching and walking has done wonders for my mental state. I glance over. She's still sitting in the corner, muttering somewhat incoherently. I wonder if she's really as catatonic as the others think she is. It seems like she wants to speak. Maybe she just doesn't know how. Or doesn't remember. I don't know how I can help her at this point. I sit back down in my chair and start sketching on the notepad. It's a trick I like to use when I'm stressed. Whenever I need to get my mind off a situation, I'll pull out some paper and practice drawing the alphabet. I pick some kind of theme and try to work my way through all twenty-six letters. I don't remember where it came from; I just know that, most of the time, it works. I used this trick a lot when I was working on my PhD, juggling work and my duties as a teacher.

    I'm not sure why I took the job at Crestview Middle School. I guess I thought teaching English to a bunch of thirteen and fourteen year olds would be easy and give me plenty of time to focus on my thesis. It was small town filled with families who weren't millionaires but weren't exactly struggling either. I thought it would be easy enough to go unnoticed. What I forgot to think about was how tired I would be.

My hat's off to all those who manage to keep teaching after the first year. I certainly don't have that kind of will power. One year was all I could take. Even if it was just eighth grade, those students much more manageable than others, I wasn't cut out for that life. Sure, I was teaching English and I had a little more freedom with my curriculum than my fellow faculty but I was young. I didn't want to be a teacher. I wanted something more glamorous, more 'merit worthy'. I had two degrees in psychology and law. I was close to being PhD certified! And here I was, teaching English to eighth graders to get by.

I suppose my attitude was the source of most of my problems. Yes, I made sure my students had something to occupy their time in class, lectured them a little here and there but I didn't actually teach much. In my mind, I was there for one year, just long enough to gain my title and leave as quickly as possible. I graded haphazardly, often only glancing at the first pages of essays before slapping a grade on the top and moving on. I secretly prayed there would be no questions and answered the ones I got as fast as I could. I'm surprised the administration let me teach for a whole year. I was even more surprised when they asked me to stay for another. Of course, I turned them down. I was a doctorate by that point; I thought it was time for a real job. Little did I know just how *real* the job I ended up in would be.

13

She's still muttering. I try to pay attention to the words she's speaking but I can't make heads or tails of them. Most of the words I can't even make out. A couple I understand, words like "school" or "home" but they don't make any sense to me. Although I think I heard her say "knife" once, maybe a reference to her family's murder? If I try to listen to her for too long, it gives me a headache. She speaks so quietly it's almost as though a ghost is whispering to me. She even kind of looks like one too with her dark hair hanging limply over a fragile body. Her clothes look like they're swallowing her. For some strange reason I feel like this ghost has been sent to me for some kind of punishment. Like poor old Ebenezer Scrooge and his ghosts of Christmas. Only I know this ghost will haunt me forever. Just like my mother.

14

I've only ever seen my mother once since running away. It was after school one day. I had lingered at Crestview, in tutorial, longer than I meant to and was in a hurry to get home; the clouds overhead weren't particularly inviting and I'd forgotten my raingear. I was walking out of the school with my student—don't ask me who because I honestly can't remember. I recall trying to find a way to leave without seeming rude. I believe I said something along the lines of, "It was great to see you in tutorial today. Come by and see me any time you have questions. I'll be there if you need me." What a lie, but I was finally able to shake off the student. As I walked past a crop of trees next to Crestview, an old woman with a blue bicycle suddenly appeared and started walking towards me. At first I paid her no attention; all I could think about was how much I didn't want to get caught in the storm. I could feel her watching me as I stared at the sky, praying for the clouds to hold off. When she came close enough to shake hands with, however, I realized she looked familiar. I stopped in my tracks as she passed by and turned around slowly.

"Mom?" I ventured carefully, not sure if she would even hear me. I swear I have never seen a person jump higher in my life. I was turned all the way around by this point and I saw her body stiffen over the rusty bike.

"Abby Amherst?" I said again. Her shoulders began to shake and her head began to dip down into her chest. I took a step forward and raised my hand to touch her on the shoulder when she turned her head slowly. I opened my mouth to say something but the words died in my throat as I gazed at her face, horrified. Her eyes burned into mine and in them I saw the accusations, the hurt, the insanity that drove her over the edge. I barely recognized the person I once knew as my mother. It's as though someone had taken her eyes, melted them, burned them and then thrown them carelessly back into her head. I saw a glimmer of recognition accompanied by a sort of agony and fury. We stood like this for a minute or two until she whipped her head back around, leapt on the bike with more agility than I would have given her credit for, and pedaled away, leaving me far behind.

I continued home, shaken from the encounter, but determined to put it out of my head. I made myself dinner (which I hardly ever do) and even read all of my students' papers in their entirety while the rain pounded on the windows. After several essays, I could feel the memory of my mother fading. I thought that was the end of it. I should have known better.

15

I'm starting to think these aren't just random mutterings. Several times now I've heard the same four words very clearly. She keeps repeating, "school," "teacher," "home," and "knife," with pauses after each one. They're the only intelligible words I can make out. I can't shake the feeling that there's more meaning to them. Like they're all connected somehow. It's frustrating that I can't figure them out but at least it puts my notepad to good use.

16

The next day at school was the worst. For all of us. It wasn't the worst because of what had happened but because no one had been told anything yet. Classes were cancelled for the students but all the teachers were called in for an emergency meeting, without being told the purpose. People congregated in empty hallways and secluded corners of the school, trying to figure out what had happened. Rumors flew around campus, each one contradicting another. Some claimed that there had been a fire, others that the storm last night had killed someone at the school, and so on.

I missed most of this. Apparently I was of special interest; I was sequestered in a small break room with just the detectives assigned to the case. I had no idea why. I remember answering question after question for them but never getting to ask any of my own. Finally, I snapped.

"Will someone *please* tell me what the hell is going on?!" I exclaimed in frustration. The room went quiet very quickly. After a few moments, a dark skinned man stood up from his chair and walked closer to me.

"Last night," he said slowly, as though unsure of where to begin, "Mary Robinson's family was attacked and murdered by an unknown intruder." I sagged in my chair and felt all the air leave my body. I put my hands over my eyes. Someone squeezed my shoulder. The dark skinned detective cleared his throat quietly.

"We understand Mary was your student," he continued, "so we're asking you these questions because we're hoping you might be able to help us." I shook my head and looked up.

"I swear I don't have a clue about the murder or her or anything," I began but the detective cut me off.

"That's not what I meant," he said then paused uncomfortably. I motioned for him to continue.

"Well, uh, it seems Ms. Robinson is our only witness," he explained.

"It *seems*?" I cut in. He coughed.

"Uh, my mistake," he corrected. "She is our only witness but she, uh, she's experienced, uh, some severe…mental incapacitation due to, uh, shock." I exhaled heavily and ran my hands through my hair, closing my eyes.

"What about neighbors, people in the street? Didn't anybody hear the screaming? I mean who called the police for god's sake?" I demanded, still struck by disbelief. I could hear the other detectives shifting around me.

"Well," said the dark skinned man, "it seems several of the houses in the Robinsons' neighborhood are for sale and, thus, empty for the time being. And no one was in the street due to the overcast weather." I sighed heavily and rubbed my eyes with the palms of my hands.

"So, uh," the detective began again after a respectable pause, "we've found out from some of her friends that you were her favorite teacher and that you have a degree in psychology so…" He trailed off and looked around for help. Another of his colleagues, the only female in the room, continued.

"So we thought you might be able to help us work with her," she said in a brisk, business-like tone. I remember shaking my head for a very long time at this point.

"I'm pretty sure there are others out there much more qualified than I am," I said finally. "Just because I have a degree in psychology doesn't mean I have the slightest clue about how to deal with a mental murder witness." The dark skinned detective nodded in understanding.

"Normally, yes, we would find a professional with experience in this field," he replied, "but we think normal therapy might not work so well in this case. So we've decided to try something called interpersonal psychotherapy. Have you heard of it?"

"Vaguely," I nodded, trying to recall my psych classes. "Doesn't it have to do with social associations?" He nodded.

"The reason we've come to you instead of a professional," he continued, "is because you not only have a personal connection with the witness but you also have an understanding, however slight, of the methods we use." I sat pensively for a few moments.

"I still don't think I'm going to be of any help," I started slowly. "I mean, yes, I am planning to work in this field after I receive my PhD but I'd hardly consider myself a viable candidate this early in the game. Her mental…incapacitation might wear off in a few days."

"You're still better than nothing," commented one of the other detectives from the back of the room.

"I seriously doubt that," I replied, slowly getting frustrated. "Yeah, I get it, I have an understanding of the…methods. But there are plenty of other people who can help you with this, people who are probably in a much better mental state than someone, like me, who just found out that their student's family was murdered! Did you ever think that maybe I'm not totally—"

"We realize this a difficult situation for you," interrupted the female detective, "but it's hard for all of us and we'd appreciate it if you would deal with your problems on your own time. Now, the most important thing is doing whatever we can to help each other, right?" Her patronizing tone cut straight through my numb shock and released the anger behind it. I'm still not entirely sure what I said, the details are hazy, but it definitely involved a lot of shouting on my part. It ended with the female detective being escorted out of the room by the others. As I settled back into my chair, the dark skinned detective laid a hand on my shoulder and leaned over to place a card on the table. I braced myself for another plea for help but all he said was, "If you need to talk. The name's Geahring. Sean Geahring." He straightened and walked out the door, leaving me alone with my thoughts.

After the mess with the detectives, I spent the rest of the academic year in a subdued state. So did most of the rest of the school. We were still coming to terms with what had happened. After eighth grade graduation, I packed my things and left, eager to put Crestview behind me. I'd finished my PhD work and had received a job offer in the field of clinical psychology, specifically as a therapist for witnesses involved in traumatic crimes. I started off in a more administrative position, a sort of apprenticeship, until I built up enough experience and reputation to be given cases of my own. I threw myself into my work, trying to replace the confusing and unpleasant memories in my head with the details from each case I worked on. Eventually, after two years, I only had distant memories of Crestview and Mary Robinson. And I never heard from Geahring or any of the other detectives assigned to the case again. Until now.

Two days ago, I was filling out paperwork in my office when a call came in. It was the detective.

"Dr. Amherst?" he began. "I'm not sure if you remember me—"

"I do," I answered curtly. "Unfortunately, I remember most everything from that…case." He coughed lightly in response.

"Well, that makes my job easier," he continued. "The case hasn't yet been closed and we're in need of a specialist with your qualifications." I suddenly got a bad feeling and came very close to hanging up right then and there.

"Go on," I replied. He cleared his throat and coughed again.

"The witness, if you remember, is still, uh, catatonic," he explained. "I understand you've had experience with subjects like this before." I nodded before realizing he couldn't see me.

"Yes," I said, voice cracking slightly. "Yes, I've worked with witnesses in similar mental states before. What do you need me to do?" There was a long pause. Some shuffling of paper.

"We need you to come in and take a look at her," he said. "We've had four other psychologists attempt to treat her but she has remained unresponsive. It seems like no one is able to get her to remember anything about what happened." I blinked several times before replying.

"Did you just say four?" I managed weakly.

"Yes," he replied. "Four. And we're almost out of options here." I shook my head.

"Detective Geahring, you do realize that, in my business, a witness who fails three specialists is considered to be a lost cause, right?"

"I know but," he paused, "but I can't close the case like this. It just wouldn't feel right." I shook my head again and sighed. I even lowered the phone from my ear for a moment. There was a kind of desperation in his voice that surprised me. I couldn't fathom why Geahring was so set on solving the case. There were tens of cases that came through our offices every day that went unsolved. Why was this case so special?

"Detective Geahring," I said slowly, "understand that I can't promise you anything. Even if I do come in, I will most likely achieve about the same amount of success as the four before me. This case may not have the nice, clean ending you want." He coughed again.

"I understand," he replied, "but I'd still appreciate it if you gave it a shot."

"…Fine. Where do I need to be?"

"I'll send someone to collect you. Don't worry about paying for transportation, we'll cover it." I placed the phone on the receiver and collapsed into my chair. I ran my hands over my face and through my hair.

"What the hell did I just do?"

17

That phone call feels like eternities ago. I remember nearly backing out of the job on the plane here. Now I can't decide whether that would have been a better idea. I run my hands through my hair in much the same way I did a couple days ago. I exhale loudly and lay my head on the desk. The muttering is still coming from the corner of the room. Those same four words show up every now and then. I raise my head a few inches to look at her. She isn't drawing a circle anymore. Now I'm sitting upright again. She isn't drawing anymore at all, in fact. She's writing something. I get up slowly, moving towards her. The letters at her feet are "A," "M" and "H". There are also three numbers, "2," "2," and "1". I've made it around the desk and take another step towards her. She freezes suddenly, in the act of slowly tracing a "C". Her eyes make their way slowly up to my face, linger for a moment then fall quickly back down to her feet. Again, those four words.

"School...teacher...home...knife..." And suddenly it hits me. What I'm supposed to say.

"School..."

"Crestview," I say. Her finger stops. Her eyes move to my feet.

"...Teacher..."

"Amherst." Her hand curls into a fist. Her eyes move to my knees.

"...Home..."

"221 Brook Ave," I recite, remembering the note in her case file. Her eyes move to my neck and chest.

"...Knife..."

"…Murder…" I answer reluctantly. There is a long pause as her eyes make their way slowly to my face. I see a single tear run down her cheek. The silence stretches on until—

"……blue…blue bike…" And suddenly I can't breathe.

PART TWO

74

18

"It was great seeing you today, Mary. Come by any time. I'll be there if you need me." The words echo in her head as she walks down the street towards her home. She tries to halt the smile from spreading across her face but can't stop it from happening. It's getting dark and she knows she shouldn't have stayed after school as long as she did but she couldn't help it. It's not every day she gets to spend a whole tutorial with her favorite teacher all to herself. She hugs her books closer to her chest and slows her walk, trying to remember everything he said.

"That was a nice essay you wrote Mary."
"I enjoyed your comments in class today

Mary." "You should speak up more Mary, your classmates might learn something." She smiles again. Mr. Amherst is the best, as all her friends have heard countless times. They stopped taking her seriously a while ago. But they just don't get it, she thinks, they've never had him as a teacher. Who else lets students have free "creative days" to write whatever they want? And she's pretty sure the other teachers aren't as attractive. She makes sure to check his outfit every day so she can remember what he was wearing if anything special happens. She knows her friends think she's obsessed but who better to be obsessed with? At least it's not some brainless pop star. Grinning, she imagines Mr. Amherst telling the whole class how smart she is. She imagines receiving one of his smiles, meant just for her. She can see his face, his dark brown hair falling casually onto his forehead and his bright blue eyes winking quietly at hers. She grins in embarrassment, even though there's no one around to see, and sheepishly tucks her hair behind her ears. Emerging from her fantasies, she realizes she's passed her house already. She turns back and tries to wrestle the grin off her face before she reaches the unlocked back door. She doesn't want her parents or her brother asking any nosy questions, like they always do. She heads through the back gate towards the door, too preoccupied with her thoughts to notice the squeaking hinges announcing a second person passing through the gate behind her. Reaching the house and confident that her face is sufficiently devoid of any embarrassing emotions, she opens the door to step inside.

"Dad! Mom! I'm home!" she yells, dropping her backpack and books on the floor.

"Hey, in the kitchen," her father replies from further inside the house. "Your mom's upstairs with Cameron."

"As she always is," she says back, smiling. She can hear her father's laugh.

"Well," he says after a moment, "I hope you like hamburgers because that's what's for dinner tonight." She smiles at her father's joke; he knows hamburgers are her favorite meal. She heads down the hallway towards the living room. She hears her father's steps as he comes into the room to meet her.

"Hey Da—" she stops at the sound of the screen door banging shut, staggering footsteps and heavy breathing behind her. She freezes and turns slowly, praying it's just her brother playing a joke on her. As she turns to face whoever is behind her, she hears her father's voice, booming through the house.

"MARY, GET DOWN! NOW!" But she can't move. Behind her is an old woman holding a long knife, poised to strike. She screams but her voice dies halfway through it as she finds herself staring into the most terrible eyes she's ever seen. They look as though they were once made of wax but disfigured beyond recognition. She can see faint traces of blue but a bloodshot red mostly obscures them. She recoils at the fury in them and is confused by the accusation behind it. She can hear her father moving towards her. Suddenly the woman is shouting incoherently and Mary falls to the floor. She watches in horror as the woman swings the knife around and lets go, launching it with incredible speed at her father, catching him by surprise. She wants to run but she can't. Her fear has her rooted to the floor against the wall. She can't scream as her father falls to the ground, the knife sticking out of his neck. All she can do is watch as the woman wrenches the dagger out of the now still body of her father. Suddenly, her mother and brother come running into the hallway, drawn by all the noise. They freeze at the sight of the woman and her father's body. Mary watches her mother lean against the wall and slide down it, her eyes fixated on the body and the blood. The old woman screams again and attacks, driving the knife into the immobilized form of Elizabeth Robinson. Mary watches in horror as her younger brother tries to stop the assault and ends up on the ground next to her family. She watches as the woman rises unsteadily from the carnage, no longer shouting. The woman looks up at Mary, still frozen on the ground in shock and fear. Her eyes don't even look human anymore as they find their way to Mary's face. The woman raises the bloody knife slowly and points it at Mary. Then she speaks.

"He…promises," she says, her words punctuated by heavy breaths. "He promises. To be there. If you…need him. Liar. He's…lying to you. He'll leave you. They all…leave you." Mary nods in fear, unsure of what to do, unsure of what do say. The woman bears her teeth and squeezes her eyes shut. Suddenly she's yelling again.

"LIAR! HE'S A LIAR! HE'LL LEAVE! THEY ALWAYS LEAVE! THEY ALWAYS! LEAVE! ME!" Mary tries to close her ears against the noise but can't get her hands to move. The woman shrieks incoherently and runs wildly towards Mary. Her heart stops as the woman reaches her but she blows past, knocking the screen door off its hinges. Mary watches the woman make her way through the back yard and the last thing she notices as she blacks out is the murderer clambering onto an old, rusted blue bike.

19

It's dark here. And cold. She sees shapes and maybe faces—but she can't be sure. Nothing makes sense. She covers her ears and moans. Suddenly there are hands on her arms, noises in her ears. She shakes her head and moans again, staring at the ground. Suddenly she's being moved. Put somewhere, told something. She can't breathe, can't think. Everything goes black again but she can still feel. Words break through to her every once in a while. Words like "shock" and "hospital" and "help." She doesn't understand. For a while she manages to shut everything out.

20

How much time has passed? She can't remember. All she sees are dark rooms and white hair and low voices. Sometimes the voices are alone. Sometimes they bring food. Other times they bring people and lights. She never says anything. She knows she's being asked questions. Being told important things. She can't speak. She realizes she doesn't remember how.

21

There's a new voice now. But it hasn't had much to say. Just one word but she can't remember what it was. She wonders if she can ignore him like the others. She waits for him to ask questions. But he never does. He just sits there. She crouches against the walls, braced for the voice. It never comes. Time passes, she begins to relax. Then he shifts, he moves. She braces herself again but, still, the voice doesn't come. She raises her head slowly. He's staring at her. And she knows that stare.

22

Drawing circles calms her. She watches her feet and her circles, slow and in control. She wants to block out what happened. She doesn't want to raise her head again. The voice still hasn't come. She wonders why he won't speak. Something nags at her mind, some reason for his silence. She pushes it away but it comes back. She ignores it but it gets louder. She can't understand it; she doesn't know what it's saying, doesn't want to. There's too much noise in her head now. She retreats back into her mind, away from the circles, the voice and the room. The dark and the cold are comforting, familiar. She doesn't remember how she got here.

23

She can feel his eyes again. He's just watching her draw circles. Do circles help him too? Her eyes long to look up again but she won't let them. That's dangerous, she says to them, you shouldn't want to look. The odd thing is she can feel her mouth moving along with her words. And it keeps moving. She realizes this is important. She remembers something about her mouth. She's supposed to use it for a reason. But what was the reason?

24

Now she can hear a voice but it's not his voice. It must be hers. She can't understand what her voice wants to say. Words float around in her mind but she pushes them away. Let her mouth deal with them; it seems to know what to do. She keeps drawing the circle as four words decide to hover behind her eyes. She tries to push them back like the others. She pauses in her drawing because they won't go away.

"School." The word sounds familiar in her ears.

"Teacher." She remembers that one too.

"Home." She sees an image for a moment, a small house in a small neighborhood.

"Knife." She sees red and her finger begins tracing again, only this time she isn't tracing a circle anymore. She looks down again. Letters. She's drawing letters.

"Teacher." she says again and her finger begins tracing an "A."

25

He's watching her again. She keeps drawing her letters and repeating those four words every now and then. They mean something, she knows, she just can't decide what. She now has six figures. Three letters and three numbers. A, M, H, 2, 2 and 1. She doesn't know what they mean.

"School." Now her finger is tracing a "C." Her eyes catch a movement in front of the room. He's walking towards her. She stops drawing and her eyes move up to his face. She watches his eyes for a moment and then drops her gaze back to her feet.

"School…teacher…home…knife…" She wants to keep drawing but she can't.

"School…"

"Crestview." The voice echoes loudly in her head, familiar but foreign at the same time. She blinks and her eyes move towards it. She focuses on a pair of dark shoes. C…

"…Teacher…"

"Amherst." Her eyes move slowly up to knees encased by dark, loose fitting slacks. A…M…H…

"…Home…"

"221 Brooke Avenue." She's watching his chest now, covered by a dark shirt and jacket. 2…2…1…

"…Knife…"

"…Murder…" The black is gone. The cold is gone. She's looking at his face now and in his eyes she can see her parents, her brother. She can hear a woman's shriek. She can feel a child's fear. She can see—

"……blue…blue bike…" And suddenly she can breathe again.

PART THREE

26

I'm still not sure what happened that day. I mean I know what happened as far as physical events go. It's what went on inside that I don't quite understand.

It may have taken two years and twenty-one hours but, somehow, Mary Robinson's case was finally closed. The authorities found my mother's body bundled up in an abandoned apartment complex, lifeless. They think she'd been dead for several months now. They also found what appeared to be the remains of a rusted blue bike and a long, serrated knife.

Mary's begun speaking again and is slowly regaining her ability to function in regular society. In the times that I've visited her, she seems to be taking to rehabilitation very nicely. Our conversations are amicable and she looks as though she enjoys them. We just don't talk about anything from before. Her problems aside, I'm not sure I could handle speaking about those memories yet. The doctors are confident she'll be ready to rejoin the real world soon. I'm glad. She deserves a chance to start over.

27

I met up with Detective Geahring not long after the case was closed and Mary had been settled into rehab. I'd meant to ask him why he'd pushed so hard to solve this murder.

"John Robinson was a good friend of mine from our college days," he explained over lunch. "We both wanted to join the police force when we graduated and we did, but John never seemed to like it as much once we got there. Didn't surprise me when he quit to start a family."

"How long were you in the force together?" I asked.

"Only about four or five years, I think," he replied. "John became disillusioned pretty quickly."

"Did you stay in touch after he left?" I asked.

"We tried to," he answered. "He'd invite me 'round for dinner to see the family every now and then and I'd take him out for drinks but we started to grow apart. Especially after I became a detective." I nodded, picking at my place absentmindedly. After a moment, I asked, "How well did you know Mary?" He stopped in the act of raising his glass for a drink.

"I knew her from the day she was born," he said quietly. "I used to babysit when John wanted to go out with Elizabeth. She and I got along great. She even used to call me Uncle Sean…" His voice dropped away and we spent the next couple minutes in silence, staring at our plates. I made a half-hearted comment about the weather to try and break the silence but Geahring gracefully ignored it. We spent another few minutes listening to the TV playing at the bar of the restaurant. I was about to suggest we pay and split when he lifted his head to stare out the window.

"I guess I just always thought I would be the first to go," he said, watching the life outside pass us by.

28

As for me, I've quit the business of psychotherapy. I've realized I'm not cut out for that sort of work. Instead, I'm back where I belong: teaching English classes at a small high school in a small town. I teach tenth grade now, those students so much less manageable than my eighth graders. So much nosier too. Their favorite distraction game is to ask me about my past. I guess my convoluted history was good for something after all. I hope they're as entertained by my stories as I think they are. More importantly, I hope I'm teaching them to appreciate what they have, something I learned from Mary during those twenty-one hours. Throughout my life, I strove to forget everything from my past: my family, what I'd been through, even parts of my life with old man Grumman. I thought that forgetting was the only way I could move forward. Boy, was I wrong. After spending that time with Mary, I've learned the only way I can move on with my life is if I start facing my history and dealing with it in the present. I still remember the last thing I said to her as we collapsed into each other's arms, the weight of the world too much for both of us at that moment. As her tears ran down my shirt and mine down my cheeks, I leaned towards her ear.

"Thank you."

EPILOGUE

29

Standing outside the tall, white building, I fight the urge to turn around and walk away. I can see an officer beckoning me inside but decide to ignore him for a moment. I take a few sips from my coffee and go over everything I want to say a couple times. Finally, I toss the cup in the trashcan and make my way inside.

"Hey, what took you so long?" the waving guard asks. "I've been waiting for you. I kept trying to catch your attention."

"Oh really? Sorry, I couldn't see you," I lie as he leads me deeper into the building.

"No problem," he says. "I just didn't want you freezing your butt off outside." He speaks with the sort of animation that belies inexperience so I figure the kid is new to the job. I wonder briefly what would happen to him after a couple years, when I notice he's stopped in front of a large black door.

"He's just through there," chirps the young guard. I nod as he spins around to leave and wait until his footsteps have faded to step inside.

"Mikey?" I freeze as the familiar voice washes over me and the door slams shut. I can't stop staring at the face in front of me. It's a face I haven't seen since I was fifteen years old. I stand, body tensed, for a moment until his face breaks into a timid smile.

"Hey," he says. "It's been a while." I let out my breath and relax, dropping into the seat across the table from my brother. He's older and more worn but I can still see the Shane I remember.

"Yeah," I reply. "Sorry." He shakes his head.

"What are you apologizing for?" he asks. I shrug my shoulders weakly.

"For running." My brother shakes his head again.

"I don't blame you for wanting to get out," he says. "If I'd had the guts, I would have gone with you probably." I stare at him, not quite willing to believe my ears yet. He laughs softly.

"Kind of hard to believe isn't it?" he says. "After what we did to you back then." Now it was my turn to shake my head.

"That was a long time ago," I replied quietly. "A lot has changed since then."

"A lot *has* changed, hasn't it?" he comments, staring at the table. I'm not sure what to say to that so I stare at the table too.

"So tell me, Mikey," he begins after a minute, "what have you been up to all these years?" I look up but I can't figure out the look on his face. I pause then proceed to tell him basically everything that happened to me since I ran out. It takes almost two hours. But when I get to the part about Mary and our mother, something stops me. I don't feel like I can bring all that up just yet. It doesn't feel like either of us is ready for that discussion. When I stop talking, I notice how dry my throat has become. I almost want to ask the posted guard for a glass of water. Shane beats me to it. Surprisingly, the guard responds to our request and radios for the water. As we're waiting for our drinks, my brother speaks.

"That's a pretty impressive story," he says. "A hell of a lot more impressive than mine, anyways." I stare at my brother for a moment.

"What exactly happened to everyone?" I finally ask. "I know the details from the court records but…" His eyes meet mine over the table.

"The records are pretty much everything," he said. "We made a mistake, the biggest anyone could possible make. We murdered two people we didn't even know for a stupid, stupid reason and, eventually, we're all going to pay for it. Mark and Kevin have. Now I'm the only one left." He stops talking for a moment and I think he's finished. Our waters have finally arrived so I reach out to take a sip when he speaks again.

"It's not so surprising really," he says, "how we all ended up. After what we put you through all those years." I make an odd sound in my throat, something between a grunt and a cough. He catches my eyes again.

"I've always wanted to apologize," he says, "for what we did to you. It wasn't right. It wasn't fair." I try to shrug my shoulders like it's all behind me but I can't bring myself to do it. Because I know what he's saying is true.

"I've spent a lot of time trying to think of a reason for why we beat on you so much," he continues, "but everything I come up with just sounds like a bad excuse. At least in my case. Kevin, I know, just enjoyed violence. I was too afraid not to follow along.

"Mark was different though. I think he realized that, of all of us, you were the only one who had a shot of making it out alive. I think that's why he tried so hard to beat you down. Because he wanted you to learn how to take a hit. You know, after you left I used to catch him smiling for no apparent reason. I think he was smiling because he knew you were out there, somewhere, fighting back." I'm not sure what to say in response to this and Shane seems to understand.

"I know it's probably too little too late," he says, "but I really am sorry about what we did to you. I always felt bad afterwards, but I was too frightened of Mark and Kevin to say anything. I wish I had. I mean, if I'd spoken up maybe—"

"No," I cut in sharply. Shane stops and watches me with a confused look. "It...that's all in the past now. We can't change what we did." He opens his mouth to speak again but I beat him too it.

"Yeah, you guys made my life a living hell," I say, "and I lived my life in utter fear of what you were going to do next. But if you hadn't done that, I never would have run away. I never would have had a chance to get to where I am today. I owe you for that at least." Shane drops his gaze to his knees and I busy myself with my water, feeling a little awkward and not entirely sure where all that came from. After a minute or two, his voice creeps out from behind his hair.

"Never thought I'd see you again," he murmurs, "and I definitely didn't think I'd hear you thanking me for what I did."

"And I never thought I'd have the guts to come back here and say that," I reply. "I almost turned around and went home when I was standing outside." He chuckles softly.

"Too bad Mark and Kevin aren't here to enjoy this lovely little reunion," he adds and I notice the sharp edge to his voice.

"…What happened?" I ask finally. Shane chuckles again.

"Prison happened," he answers, "but I suppose that's what we get for what we did. I'm just surprised I wasn't the first to die. To be fair, Kevin's death wasn't all that much of a shock. I always thought his liking for violence would get him in the end.

"Mark's was tougher to take though," he explains after a pause. "I always looked up to him as the leader, the strong one in the family. When we were kids, people used to think the three of us were scary as hell but really it was Mark they were frightened of. Kev and I were just his loyal guard dogs.

"That's why I don't buy the "official" suicide story. I don't think Mark killed himself because he couldn't take the prison life. I think he killed himself because he figured his job was done. He didn't have to look out for me and Kev anymore and he hadn't had to worry about you for years. I guess he wanted to quit while he was ahead." I realize I've been nodding during his speech and try to hold my head still.

"Maybe that's why I'm still here," he continues, "because I know I'm not finished yet. The guilt is still too strong."

"The kids?" I ask softly. He nods.

"I know we didn't mean to kill 'em, or at least I didn't, but that doesn't change the fact that we did," he says. "People in here talk about biding their time until they get out but I'd rather just stay. In here, I can't think about anything but what I did wrong all those years ago." I realize he's not just talking about the murder but me as well.

"That's the real punishment in jail," he remarks. "They don't sentence you to serve years locked up with other criminals. They sentence you to serve years trapped with your own mind."

"You don't have to be in jail to be trapped by your mind," I say and he looks at me with skepticism. "In fact, I only needed twenty-one hours in a mental institution." Now he looks confused so, finally, I tell him about our mother and what she did to Mary's family. He closes his eyes and a pained look comes over his face.

"I guess none of us can escape the past," Shane says finally. I nod my head in agreement then add, "But maybe that's not such a bad thing."

Suddenly, there's a knock on the door. The guard opens it to reveal the young officer I met earlier in the morning.

"Sorry but time's almost up," he says cheerily. I turn back to my brother who still has his eyes closed. I take a card out of my pocket and lay it on the table in front of him. He opens his eyes as I stand up to leave.

"That's my address and phone number," I explain as he picks up the paper, "if you want to talk." I turn, leaving him to study the words, and make my way to the door. As I reach it, his voice calls out.

"I'm glad you turned out the way you did Mikey. Maybe there's hope for our family after all." I smile and raise my hand in a wave, turning to walk past the door. As it closes behind me I swear I can see him waving back.

118

Acknowledgements

There are so many people to thank I have no idea where to start. First of all, thank you to my family, who agreed to the crazy idea of letting me take the last month of my senior year to write a book. Mom, dad and E, I love you all.

Second, where would I be without Kim Morgan, Jonathan Newman, Deborah Watson, Bennett Spann and anyone and everyone who supports the Lovett School Senior Projects? Thank you all so much for believing I could actually pull this off and giving me the chance to do so. I really appreciate your time and your feedback because this book would never have happened if not for you help and support along the way.

And I can't forget to thank my lovely editor, Mr. Nick Mencher! Thank you for your guidance and help in turning this book into the best it could be. I don't know where I'd be without you.

Thanks to my cousin Brian Hwang for introducing me to Natalie Danford. And thanks to Natalie Danford for answering some very vital questions to help me along my way in writing.

Finally, thank you for reading this book. I hope you found it as entertaining to read as I did writing it.

About the Author

Maddi Hartley is a graduate of the Lovett School in Atlanta, GA and a current student at Harvey Mudd College in Claremont, CA. She's been reading since about the time she could talk and has always wanted to give writing a try. This is her first book.

Made in the USA
Lexington, KY
28 April 2012